Karthika Naïr

Illustrations by
Joëlle Jolivet

The Honey Hunter

LITTLE
GESTALTEN

On a day like today, in a neighborhood not far from here, at a dinner table not unlike our own, two people—quite like you and me—were engrossed in a discussion of some importance.

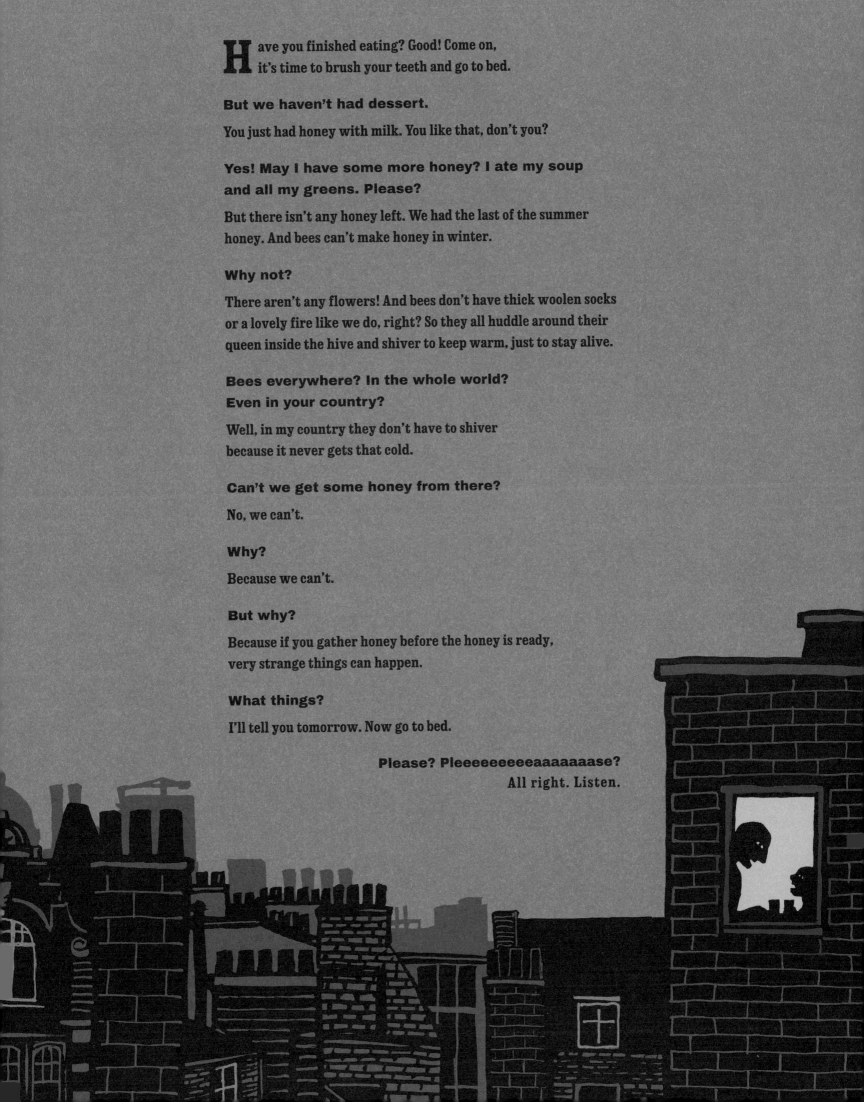

Have you finished eating? Good! Come on,
it's time to brush your teeth and go to bed.

But we haven't had dessert.

You just had honey with milk. You like that, don't you?

**Yes! May I have some more honey? I ate my soup
and all my greens. Please?**

But there isn't any honey left. We had the last of the summer
honey. And bees can't make honey in winter.

Why not?

There aren't any flowers! And bees don't have thick woolen socks
or a lovely fire like we do, right? So they all huddle around their
queen inside the hive and shiver to keep warm, just to stay alive.

**Bees everywhere? In the whole world?
Even in your country?**

Well, in my country they don't have to shiver
because it never gets that cold.

Can't we get some honey from there?

No, we can't.

Why?

Because we can't.

But why?

Because if you gather honey before the honey is ready,
very strange things can happen.

What things?

I'll tell you tomorrow. Now go to bed.

Please? Pleeeeeeeeeaaaaaaase?
All right. Listen.

In the country of eighteen tides, where three rivers—the Padma, the Meghna, and the Jamuna—meet, deep within a mangrove forest near the Bay of Bengal, there lived ...

What's a magroforess?

A *mangrove forest* is a forest that is almost upside down, with its head under water and its feet dancing in the air. The tree roots climb up instead of down, thick and tangled—yes, just like your hair if you don't comb it.

When the tides rise, all eighteen of them, when the water comes in, the trunks and branches dive under, every day, to take a bath. And when the tides fall, they appear again, fresh and sparkling, their leaves glinting like emeralds, their flowers bright.

Deep within a mangrove forest near the sea known as the Bay of Bengal, within a forest so marvelous and mysterious it is *actually* called the Sundarbans, the Forest of Beauty, there lived thousands and thousands, or maybe even gazillions, of honeybees.

All these thousands and thousands, or even gazillions, of bees were ruled by the Bee Goddess, the Queen Bee of queen bees from all the hives. She had big black eyes and pale, golden wings. When she moved, it was like the wind in the trees and the rush of the waves, like the moon around the earth, like constellations in motion. Thanks to her and her bees, flowers bloomed and fruits ripened. Thanks to them, life continued on earth.

By day, the bees gathered nectar, taking the pollen from flower to flower. They built honeycombs and filled them with honey: golden, rich honey—*liquid light,* some called it. Light you could drink in great gulps of joy.

Just imagine. Honey.
Running down trees like rivulets of sunshine, all the way down to the forest floor. All the animals and birds loved it.
The blue-eared kingfishers that looked like a moving patch of sky.
The flying foxes that leaped from tree to tree like superheroes.
The monitor lizards that could be the descendants of dinosaurs.
The golden deer.
The tiny, black ants.
The spiky porcupine.
The wild boar.

They climbed up the trees or swooped down from the air or
raced over to the forest floor to where it drip-drip-dripped
as it overflowed.

Why, the crocodile sang for joy when it sank its teeth into a chital
or a monkey that had feasted on honey!

Why, the earth itself loved honey, she lapped it up.

And then there was He-Whose-Name-Must-Not-Be-Taken who loved it so much that He wanted to keep it all for Himself. He particularly hated the honey collectors…

Who's He-Whose-Name-Must-Not-Be-Taken?

Shhhhhhh. If I say His name, He'll appear right away. We don't want that.

But WHO is He?!?

Ah, Him. The Lord of the South. Defender of the Forest. The Demon King. Say His name out loud and He appears. Then nobody—okay, almost nobody—can save you.

But there was someone who loved honey even more than Him.

Me?

No. A little boy called Shonu. He was your age, but a bit shorter than you. He had spiky black hair and a little black thread with an amulet around his neck, which was to keep him safe from—oh, from leopards and surly warthogs and angry tides and many dangerous, unnamable things in the forest.

He lived on a char—an island formed by all the things that the three rivers bring with them on their long journey to the sea. Chars appear and disappear with changes in seasons and tides and the monsoon, and the people who live there have to keep moving every time their island goes under water. And so it was with Shonu.

Did he live alone? Like Mowgli?

No, he lived with his parents: with Amma, his mother, who was a shrimp farmer, and Abba, his father. Abba was a Mawali, a honey collector. He collected honey and beeswax from the forest during the summer. Summer is when the Bee Goddess allows people to take honey, after the bees have built their homes, raised their young, and spread pollen from flower to flower.

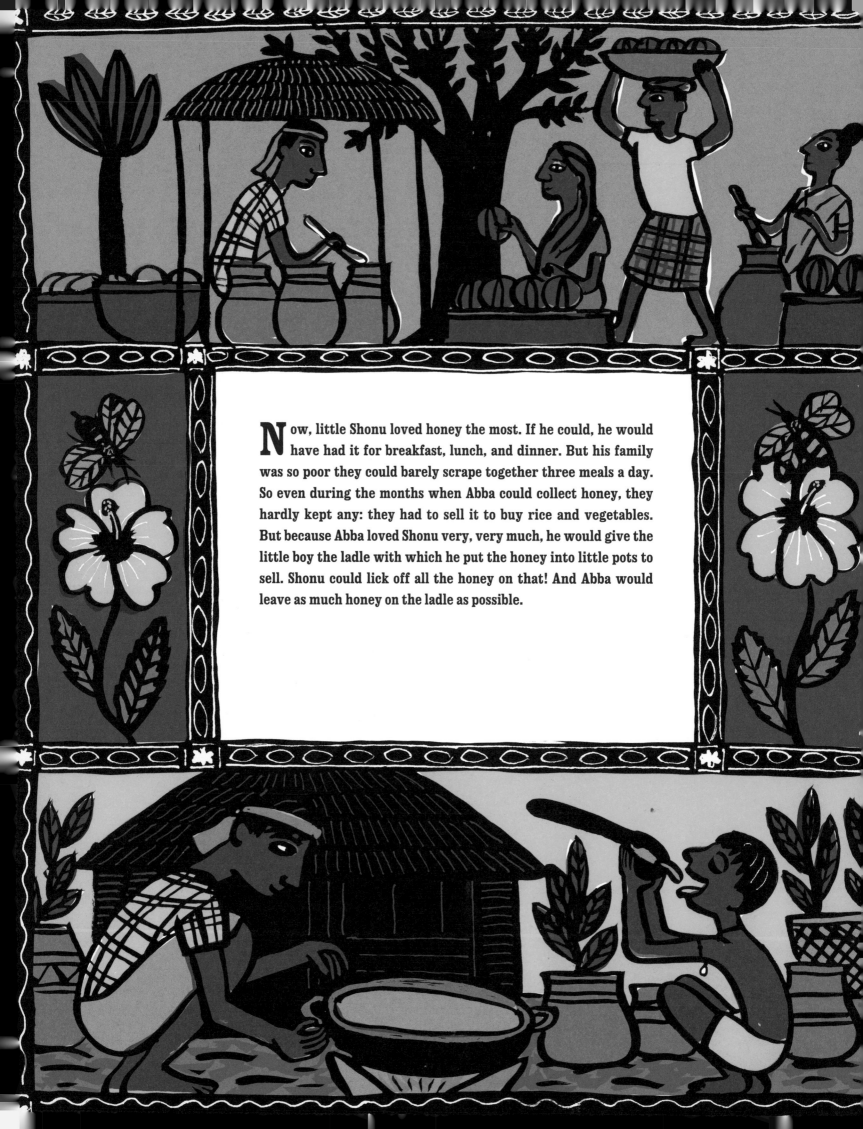

Now, little Shonu loved honey the most. If he could, he would have had it for breakfast, lunch, and dinner. But his family was so poor they could barely scrape together three meals a day. So even during the months when Abba could collect honey, they hardly kept any: they had to sell it to buy rice and vegetables. But because Abba loved Shonu very, very much, he would give the little boy the ladle with which he put the honey into little pots to sell. Shonu could lick off all the honey on that! And Abba would leave as much honey on the ladle as possible.

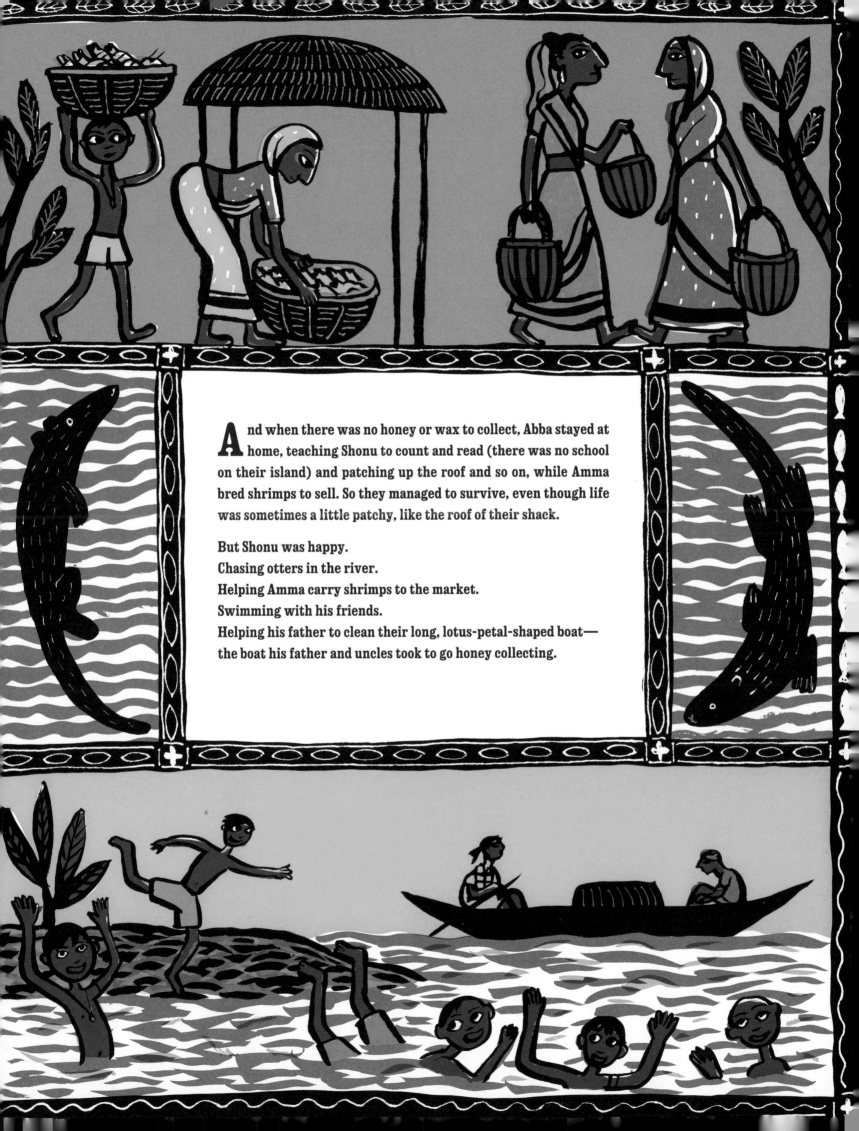

And when there was no honey or wax to collect, Abba stayed at home, teaching Shonu to count and read (there was no school on their island) and patching up the roof and so on, while Amma bred shrimps to sell. So they managed to survive, even though life was sometimes a little patchy, like the roof of their shack.

But Shonu was happy.
Chasing otters in the river.
Helping Amma carry shrimps to the market.
Swimming with his friends.
Helping his father to clean their long, lotus-petal-shaped boat—
the boat his father and uncles took to go honey collecting.

Then, one year, everything went wrong. The seasons went topsy-turvy. All six of them.

Six seasons? Not four?

Yes, the land of eighteen tides has six seasons.

Seet,
winter,

bashonto,
spring,

grishma,
summer,

and *hemanto,*
another fall, different
from the first.

borsa,
monsoon,

sarat,
fall

One after the other, just like clock-
work ... but that year, they kept
popping up out of turn. Confused and
annoyed. Like someone had mixed up
their school calendars.

Instead of a quiet, cool *bashonto*, cyclones swept in from the coast—without warning, like nightmares.

They beat down on the land, destroying houses and boats and ports, carrying away cattle and people and poultry, scaring the fish away, and blowing in disease and hunger and death.

They submerged dozens and dozens of chars, and created new ones miles away.

They ravaged the forests, uprooting trees and drowning animals.

The tides came in at all hours, making everything salty: freshwater was hard to get on some days.

Amma's shrimp farm—and all the other shrimp farms on the islands—got swept out into the sea. The fish in the rivers began to disappear.

Shonu and his family moved home three times in two months, rowing from one island to another as the waters rose. They built and dismantled, packed and unpacked their few belongings, bred shrimps and lost them.

Again
and again
and again.

January gave way to February: bashonto slunk away. And instead of tiptoeing in gently, grishma arrived early: dry, hot, and furious.

The little vegetable garden behind their new shack was shrouded with dust. The blazing red sun just dried up all the plants. One by one they withered, the green bleached into dead browns and grays.

But what did they eat then?

On good days, they would make do with a bit of fish, a handful of vegetables, and rice or roti. Dry roti: there was no ghee to make the dough soft and fluffy.

On very bad days, when there was no fish at all for Amma to catch or cook, they would eat just boiled rice with chili sauce for breakfast, and drink water the rest of the day. And they would go to bed early, hoping that the next day would be better.

Then Shonu would just close his eyes, think hard of honey, and pretend that every mouthful of water was actually a spoonful of honey. Honey with roti. Honey with rice and milk—like kheer. Honey with hilsa fish—yummm. Honey scooped out of a jar with a golpata leaf-spoon, the way you eat jam!

But dreams—even dreams so delicious—cannot fill stomachs.

Why didn't they go out in the boat to the forest and get some honey?

That's exactly what Shonu asked his father every day!

But Abba would sigh and reply, "Not yet, Shonu, the bees haven't finished building their combs, summer came too early this year. This is the time for them to prepare the coming of the young queens. We must not disturb them now. We must wait until they are ready to give."

One day, Amma explained, "Your father is right. If we take the honey now, the pact between Bonbibi and He-Whose-Name-Must-Not-Be-Taken will be broken. Then there will be neither peace nor safety, not in the forests, nor in the villages. They say the woodcutters cut down too many trees last year. That's why the cyclones were so terrible. He-Whose-Name-Must-Not-Be-Taken is very angry."

Wait, who's Bonbibi?

Ah! Bonbibi—now Shonu knew who Bonbibi was! Everyone did! Daughter of Fakir Ibrahim, Elder Sister of Shah Jongali, Bonbibi is the Guardian Deity of the Sundarbans, our Patron Saint. She came a long, long time ago from very far away—from the holy city of Medina—to do battle with the Lord of the South, to wipe out the Demon King and his army of goblins, ghouls, and ghosts. And she did. After long days and longer nights of fierce and bloody battle Bonbibi defeated Dakkhin Rai.

You took his name!
You named He-Whose-Name-Must-Not-Be-Taken!!!

Yes, and it would be dreadful, just absolutely end-of-the-world-awful BUT I also took Bonbibi's name in the very same breath. So we are all safe!

But if she killed him, then…?

O h, she didn't kill him! Did I say that? No, no. Bonbibi realized that Dakkhin Rai loved the forest more than anyone else. If he was cruel, it was only because people were invading his forest to cut it down, to plunder all the honey and kill the animals that lived there. So, instead of chopping off his head, she made him promise that he would not harm anyone who respected the forest and the creatures in it.

Like Shonu's Amma and Abba?

E xactly. But now there were lots of greedy, silly people who weren't like Shonu's parents at all. And these people had been cutting down the trees, plundering the honey, and killing the animals in the Sundarbans. And Dakkhin Rai (Bonbibi save us) was angry. Very angry indeed.

But Shonu was so hungry and so tired of waiting that his parents' warnings were soon erased from his brain. The strange summer had decided to linger. The days were as long as weeks; and the nights, why, the nights seemed endless. His ache grew.

Soon there was only one thought in his mind: honey, honey, honey, honey, honey, honey.

The word beat inside his head like the waves on the shore in high tide.

An idea grew and grew in his mind until it was high as the hills of Chittagong.

Until one morning, when the hunger for honey had spread from his stomach to his chest, his throat, his legs, his head, and his heart, crawling all over his insides like a thousand red ants, he could bear it no more. He ran down to the river and hid in the boat of a woodcutter, under the floorboards. He lay there quietly, waiting for the woodcutter to cast off. And soon, he fell asleep, his hunger drowned by the rocking of the boat.

When he woke, the sky was green: not blue, but green and brown, a sky of leaves and branches with a moving, shifting land below. He saw colors flashing, changing, disappearing ... mudskippers and fishing cats and hermit crabs, not one staying still long enough for him to be sure he had seen them.

And beneath it all, beneath the chatter of cormorants, egrets, and woodpeckers, alongside the rustle of the terrapin and the pythons, and the heavy tread of the water buffalo, he heard the music of the bees: the hum of gazillions of bees hard at work.

He followed his ears, and, with his hand on his amulet, tip-toed through the woods, taking great care not to step on dry branches or anything that looked like a sleeping crocodile.

Louder and louder grew the hum until it sounded like a symphony orchestra, complete with woodwind and brass and string sections. Shonu stepped into the kingdom of honeycombs: black and gold clouds shaped like mountains, castles, crowns, roses, towers—upside-down, sideways, and downside-up, hanging from branches, rising from hillocks, growing into hollows.

Each buzz-buzzing with a gazillion bees, building and making and gathering. All far too busy to notice this hungry little boy with eyes growing wider and shinier till they were miniature suns, and a mouth that had dropped to his knees.

Shonu forgot all his father's warnings, his mother's stories.

He just threw himself at the hives, breaking off bits and pieces, and startling the worker bees.

He ran to the nearest tree, climbed up the trunk, and broke off chunks of honeycomb, squeezing them and drinking up the falling drops.

The bees, now buzz-buzzing with rage and fear, flew out in battalions to sting him—to sting him till he turned blue. But their stingers couldn't touch Shonu, though they tried and tried. His magic amulet protected him, you see—not just from leopards and warthogs and angry tides, but from angry bees too.

Shonu drank and he ran, he ran and he drank, from one hive to another.

Then a gentle, golden voice drifted across the forest: "Child, not now: not yet. The hives are full of young bees, they will perish."

But did Shonu stop? Did he listen to the plea? No! He drank and ran and drank and ran, and he kept on drinking and running until the Bee Goddess—for it was she—cried out, her voice still golden but furious...

"CEASE THIS INSTANT!
OR

DAKKHIN RAI

WILL COME
TO PROTECT MY HIVES!"

Dakkhin Rai! Oh, no!

Oh, Bonbibi, yes! Barely had the Bee Goddess taken His name than a roar reverberated across the land. A roar torn from the earth's belly: dark, raspy with anger and hate and blood. It shattered the sea like glass and froze the animals in their tracks. Shonu, who had barely noticed the Bee Goddess's voice, heard this loud and clear.

Then he heard other, more fearsome sounds: a tread that shook the ground beneath his feet, a breath that blew leaves off the nearby trees and a slow, rising growl like the rumble of a cyclone. Shonu tumbled from the branch he was perched on, straight on top of an anthill (but the ants themselves were so petrified, not a single one had the presence of mind to bite him).

Striding towards him was Dakkhin Rai, Lord of the South, Defender of the Forest, the Demon King, He-Whose-Name-Must-Not-Be-Taken, in his favorite disguise: a Royal Bengal Tiger.

His hide flamed orange as the skies at twilight, his stripes were black as night. Larger than fear and twice as angry, eyes glinting death and a mouth wide as a cave with teeth, each a long, wicked dagger.

Now most people—like those ants on the anthill—are just paralyzed by fright when they see a Royal Bengal Tiger.
But Shonu was not most people.

Shonu fled.

He ran as though there were wings on his feet and a jet engine on his back. Behind him, the earth shuddered with each step the demon-tiger took. Faster and faster the little boy sped, until he spotted the boat, with the woodcutter in it preparing to cast off.

But just as he was about to leap over the last stretch of marsh, his foot caught on the root of a Shundori tree, and he sprawled across the forest floor, a jumble of arms and legs and panic.

He felt the hot, foul breath of Dakkhin Rai on his neck and long, steely whiskers nick his ears. With the last bit of air in his lungs, Shonu screamed, "Bonbibi, save me!"

Time ceased.
The earth paused.
The skies stilled.

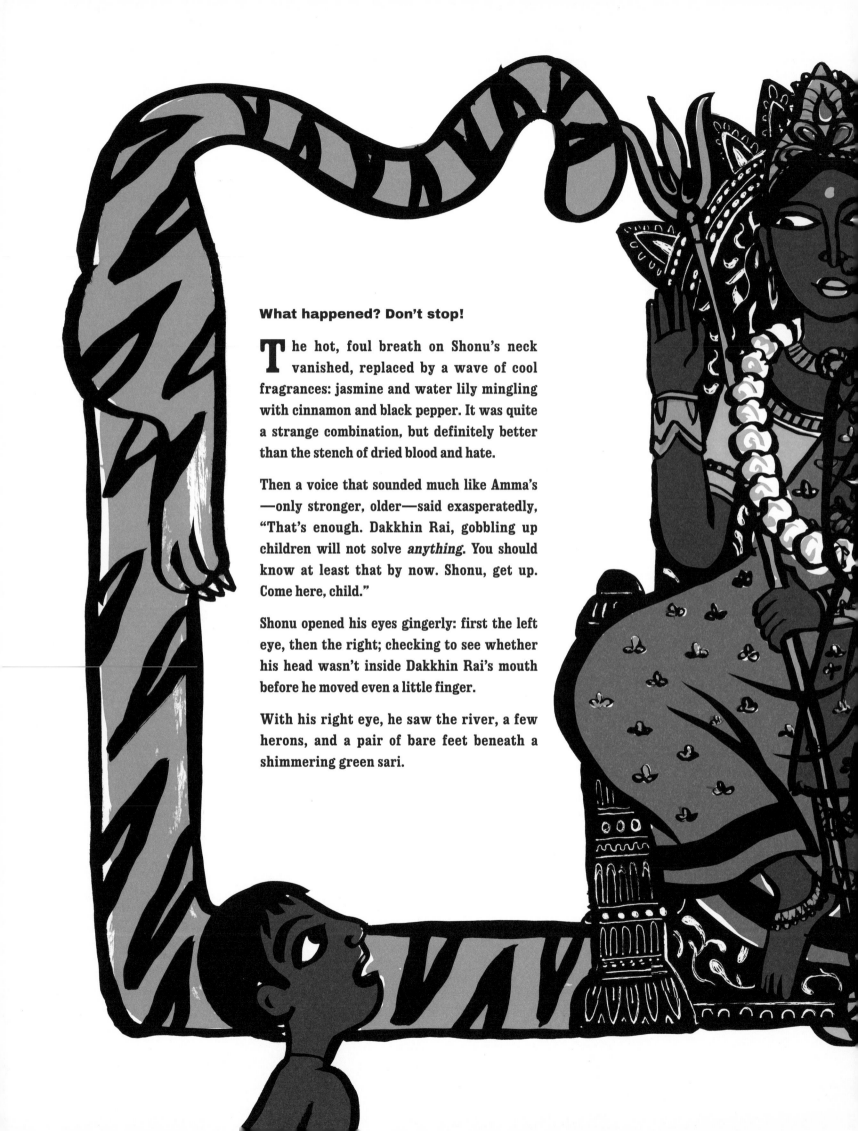

What happened? Don't stop!

T he hot, foul breath on Shonu's neck vanished, replaced by a wave of cool fragrances: jasmine and water lily mingling with cinnamon and black pepper. It was quite a strange combination, but definitely better than the stench of dried blood and hate.

Then a voice that sounded much like Amma's —only stronger, older—said exasperatedly, "That's enough. Dakkhin Rai, gobbling up children will not solve *anything*. You should know at least that by now. Shonu, get up. Come here, child."

Shonu opened his eyes gingerly: first the left eye, then the right; checking to see whether his head wasn't inside Dakkhin Rai's mouth before he moved even a little finger.

With his right eye, he saw the river, a few herons, and a pair of bare feet beneath a shimmering green sari.

Lifting his head from the mud, he saw a dark lady with a silver trident in one hand. So he opened his left eye next, and first spotted Shundori trees and buzzing bees. Then, closer still, another warrioress, in a pink salwaar-kameez and wondrously curved Persian slippers, her hair covered in a long veil.

"Another one?" he thought, "Ya-Allah! How many Bonbibis are there?"

Blinking, Shonu got up, and as he approached, he saw the two Bonbibis merge into one. Behind her paced Dakkhin Rai, still huge, still fearsome, growling and angrily lashing his flaming, striped tail.

When he saw Bonbibi bending over Shonu, wiping the child's face and hands, Dakkhin Rai roared, loud as a gale, "The boy is mine, Bonbibi. He broke the rules of the forest—now he must pay! You promised all invaders would be mine. I will crush his skull and drink his blood!"

But he didn't, did he?
Bonbibi was stronger, right?

Well, they did have a pact, you know, Bonbibi and Dakkhin Rai: she would not save any one who harmed the forest. She was stronger, oh yes, in *so* many ways. But this time, she did not fight him. She talked to him.

Bonbibi sighed, "Dakkhin Rai, I've told you already: he's just a child."

Dakkhin Rai roared again, larger and fierier, "The bees whose homes he just destroyed are *just* children too, Bonbibi! Greedy, that's what little humans are: *just* like grown-ups. Greedy. I will crush his skull and drink his blood!"

Bonbibi replied, "He was hungry, not greedy. He's been starving for weeks. Be fair. You're not well-behaved when you are starving either."

Dakkhin Rai was too angry to listen: "It's their fault we are all starving, those wretched humans! *They* cut down all the trees on the coast. *They* rob the bees. *They* kill the baby fish. That's why there are no more fruits! That's why the rivers are empty! I will crush his skull and drink his blood."

When he heard that, Shonu's heart sank deeper and deeper, until it seemed deep below the roots and the water. He hung his head in shame, thinking of all the beehives he had smashed as carelessly as the cyclone had smashed his home. He almost deserved to be eaten up, he thought, though he *really, really* hoped he wouldn't be.

Bonbibi grew stern and gentle and tall, looming over the demon-tiger: "We have all suffered, Dakkhin Rai: the animals, the plants, the humans too. Killing this child will not turn back time nor bring back the old forest. But if he makes up for the wrong he has done, there is still hope for the Sundarbans, for the bees, for him—and for you."

"Ex-excuse me, B-Bonbibi, Dakk-kkhin Rai," piped up Shonu, almost tongue-tied with nervousness, "I'm r-really, really sorr-ry I broke the b-beehives and stole the honey before it was ready. It was r-really, really wrong of me, and I understand why Dakk-kkhin Rai wants to kill me. But if there's a-anything I can do to set it right, I will. I promise."

Bonbibi smiled, and Shonu felt the ice cubes of fear clogging his throat melt. "Yes, there is, Shonu. You took something that the bees couldn't give yet, something they need right now. You must make amends: repay the bees and save the hives. But it will take time and it will not be easy. You may have to stand for months, through rain and wind and scorching sunshine. And you will be away from your family until this terrible summer is over. Can you do that?"

Dakkhin Rai growled and glowered, "But he should die for what he did! That would be justice! I will crush his skull and drink his…"

"Dakkhin Rai, I will be very angry if you go on and on! Will crushing his skull and drinking his blood save the bees? If you really want to help, stay here beside the boy and protect him!"

Dakkhin Rai quieted down, grudgingly.

What did Shonu have to do?

Shonu thought anything would be better than being eaten by a demon-tiger with hot, foul breath and teeth like wicked daggers. So he followed Bonbibi as she led him through the forest back to the kingdom of honeybees.

There, in the clearing, amidst all the hives, she told him to stand with his arms outstretched towards the sky, and promised to take him home when the rains came. Then Bonbibi touched his feet and his forehead with her silver trident and leaned down and whispered to the earth.

Shonu saw tiger ferns and mud swirl up all around him, faster and faster, until he was nothing but a kaleidoscope of green and brown. His feet began drilling into the soil, deeper and wider, seeking water, pushing pebbles out of the way, wrapping themselves around stones, and sprouting curly root hair. It was a little ticklish. He became heavier as his legs fused together into a trunk; then his chest shot upward, up, high above his head, which was tucked safely away around his tummy, now a slender, woody tummy lined with bark …

And those arms Bonbibi had asked him to stretch towards the sky? They branched into dozens of boughs. And on them grew hundreds and hundreds of eye-shaped leaves with edges like little teeth. At the end of each branch and twig was a glowing, sunshiny flower shaped like a bell. A five-petaled bell that was golden at dawn, orange by midday, and red before it faded and died.

What was it?

It was a hibiscus, the flower that bees love most. So, Shonu became a hibiscus plant: a magic one to provide a constant supply of nectar so the bees could recover the honey he had gobbled up so thoughtlessly. So they could rebuild their hives and raise their young. It was hard work to keep flowering, especially on days without rain—and they were many, for it was a horribly dry summer. Very hard work. Shonu's feet—now multiple roots—would dig deeper and deeper to suck water; the slender trunk would take all the energy up to the branches, and his leaves blazed green, drinking in the sunlight to keep the flowers blooming.

Sometimes he felt the earth shudder and heard low, raspy growls but the Demon-Tiger never showed himself. At the end of each day, Shonu was exhausted, but he couldn't even put his feet up and rest, only tuck in the leaves, fold up the flowers, and doze as best he could, standing up.

Poor Shonu!

But it was worth it. The bees, angry and hurt and doubtful at first, grew happier as the hives got repaired and rebuilt, as the young ones became bigger and stronger. At night, on their way home, they would come and tell Shonu stories. Wondrous stories of the things they had seen but also ones they had heard from their mothers. They would sing to Shonu too, songs he learned to echo with his leaves and boughs.

Then one day, the heat rose like a tidal wave and the air was so dry you could set fire to it. Shonu was stiff and bent over with thirst. His flowers were limp, the color of dried blood. The leaves crackled, parched and gray. His roots cracked. His eyes, set deep in his slender trunk, could hardly stay open, with all the bark peeling off in flakes. His thoughts went round and round in circles.

Suddenly, Dakkhin Rai strode in to the clearing, still huge and huffy and haughty. As he went over to Shonu, a flurry of questions raced through the little-boy-plant's mind:

Do demon-tigers eat wood?
Will it hurt if he breaks one of my branches?
Or bites my trunk?
What if he knocks me over?
He could, easily, couldn't he?
But didn't he promise Bonbibi?

Dakkhin Rai stood before Shonu, looked at him briefly and then shook himself. He shook and he shook and he shook. Endless showers of water—healing, fresh water from the three rivers of the land of the eighteen tides—doused Shonu: his leaves and flowers and buds and bark and trunk. It soaked the ground and trickled down into the earth, down, down to Shonu's parched roots.

Not so far away, deeper still in the forest, Bonbibi smiled.

GLOSSARY

ghee

A fat or butter made from the milk of cows and buffaloes, used in preparing all sorts of dishes, from desserts to fried rice. Boil butter until it turns liquid and clear, then strain the residue: what you get is ghee, an amber liquid with a delicious, nutty tang.

shundori
(Heritiera fomes, littoralis)

One of the commonest trees in the Sundarbans, Shundor means "beautiful one." It has egg-shaped leaves and orange-pink flowers.

modhu

Honey—of course! Written here in Bengali script.

mawali

A member of the community of traditional honey collectors in the Sundarbans. They live on chars and work in groups of seven or eight. Between the months of April and June, they set off to the forest to collect honey and wax, braving all the dangers of the Sundarbans—the biggest and scariest of which is the Royal Bengal Tiger.

MAP

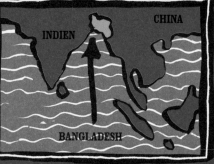

CHINA
INDIEN
BANGLADESH

Ganges
Dhaka
BURMA
BANGLADESH
Ganges Delta
Kolkata (Calcutta)
Chittagong
INDIA
SUNDARBANS
Bay of Bengal

golpata

The word actually means "a round leaf" but it isn't round at all! Golpata is the local name for the Nipa Palm, a tree we find crowding the banks of rivers and canals in the Sundarbans. Its long and slender leaves are used to make thatched roofs and walls for huts. They are also woven into baskets and spoons and other objects.

kheer

Kheer is a very popular dessert, made from rice (or wheat) cooked with milk and ghee, flavored with spices like cardamom and saffron, and garnished with cashew nuts, almonds, and raisins.

chital
(Axis axis)

One of many names of the spotted deer, an animal found in several parts of India, Bangladesh, Pakistan, Nepal, Bhutan, and Sri Lanka. It has a pale fawn coat speckled with white dots and antlers shaped like a lyre.

hilsa
(Tenualosa ilisha)

Hilsa, also known as ilish, is a very bony fish that definitely proves that looks don't matter. Ilish is much loved in Orissa, West Bengal, and Assam, and so popular in Bangladesh it was even given the title of National Fish! Unfortunately, we like ilish so much, and have eaten so much of it that it is now almost extinct in several regions.